THE CRANKY CATERPILLAR

Thames & Hudson

y and pictures by RICHARD GRAHAM

**This book is dedicated to
all those who play the pianos in
London's St Pancras train station.**

First published in the United Kingdom
in 2017 by Thames & Hudson Ltd,
181A High Holborn, London WC1V 7QX

First paperback edition 2018

Photograph of the author
by Luke Montgomery

British Library Cataloguing-in-
Publication Data
A catalogue record for this book is
available from the British Library

ISBN 978-0-500-65108-7

Manufactured in China by Imago

To find out about all our publications,
please visit **www.thamesandhudson.com**
There you can subscribe to our e-newsletter,
browse or download our current catalogue,
and buy any titles that are in print.

There wasn't much going on
when Ezra heard the noise.

The noise was grim
and **gloomy** —
a sound that
filled the room
with **blue.**

Ezra carefully walked over to the piano.

She stood on her tiptoes to look inside.

'A caterpillar!' she gasped.

This caterpillar saw Ezra and asked,

'Do you know how long I have been in here?'

'I have walked over five thousand miles in this piano', he said, 'searching for a **happy** tune. But it is useless ...

... I am **stuck** inside this piano!'

This was true.

The caterpillar had been playing the same **sad** tune for so long, he was unable to play anything else.

Round and round he played his **cranky** tune with even more **blue gloom!**

Oh how the caterpillar cried.

Worried about the cranky caterpillar,

Ezra thought some fresh air might help.

This was no good. 'TAKE ME BACK!' the caterpillar shouted. For some reason, he did not feel safe outside.

'So cranky!'

Ezra thought the caterpillar might like something to eat.

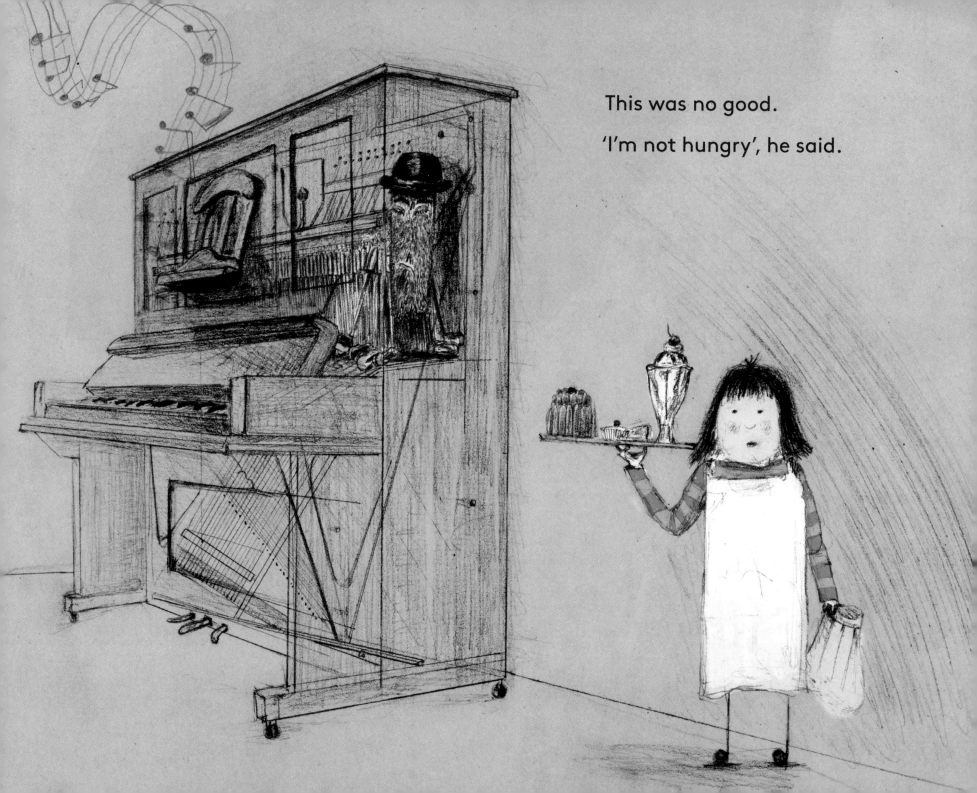

This was no good.

'I'm not hungry', he said.

She thought a new
hat might **cheer**
up the caterpillar.

This was no good either. In fact it seemed to make things **worse!**

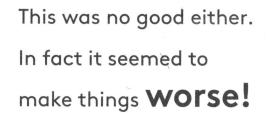

What could Ezra do to change the cranky caterpillar's tune?

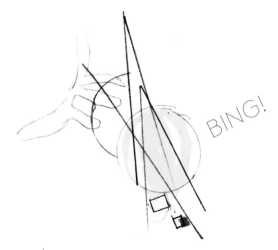

BING!

Then Ezra had a **really** **good** idea …

... she invited over some **friends!**

That afternoon Pablo Tuba, Gary Gee-tar and Wassily the Violin visited the caterpillar.

All together, they were a band!

'1, 2, 3 and...!'

Clouds of **greens, yellows**

and **oranges** began to appear.

All the colours of the rainbow

puffed into the air as the

band played. Never before

had the caterpillar heard such

happy music ! !

Suddenly a great

'BOOM!'

came from the piano.

Ezra carefully walked
over to look inside.
The caterpillar
had **disappeared!**

'Where has the caterpillar gone?'

said Gary Gee-tar.

'Why has he not said goodbye?'

said Wassily the Violin.

'It's a **mystery!**'

said Pablo Tuba.

The friends were standing in the silent room when they heard a **strange fluttering.**

'A butterfly!' Ezra said. The cranky caterpillar had turned into a **beautiful** butterfly!

The friends struck up their music once again,

as the butterfly **danced** and **sang** with joy;

'Thank you for helping me change my tune!'